D1317826

I AM THE DOG

I AM THE CAT

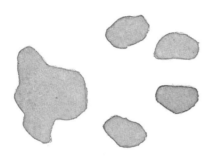

Donald Hall

I AM THE DOG

I AM THE CAT

Pictures by Barry Moser

DIAL BOOKS · New York

Published by Dial Books
A Division of Penguin Books USA Inc.
375 Hudson Street
New York, New York 10014

Text copyright © 1994 by Donald Hall
Pictures copyright © 1994 by Barry Moser
All rights reserved
Designed by Barry Moser
Printed in the U.S.A.
First Edition
10 9 8 7 6 5 4 3 2 1

Library of Congress Cataloging in Publication Data
Hall, Donald, 1928–
I am the dog, I am the cat / by Donald Hall ;
pictures by Barry Moser.—1st ed.   p.   cm.
Summary: A dog and a cat take turns explaining what
is wonderful about being who they are.
ISBN 0-8037-1504-8 (trade)
ISBN 0-8037-1505-6 (library)
[1. Dogs—Fiction.   2. Cats—Fiction.]
I. Moser, Barry, ill.   II. Title.
PZ7.H14115Iaac 1994   [E]—dc20   93-28060   CIP   AC

The illustrations were painted with transparent watercolor on paper handmade for the Royal Watercolor
Society by Simon Green. They were then color-separated
and reproduced as red, blue, yellow, and black halftones.

E Hal
Hall, Donald, 1928-
I am the dog, I am the cat

For Ariana and Abigail
D.H.

For Nancy Willard, with love
B.M.

TULSA CITY-COUNTY LIBRARY

Dog: I am the dog.
I like bones.
I like to *bury* bones.
As for eating, I can take it or leave it—
but I like it when *they* feed me.

CAT: I am the cat.
I don't *care* whether they feed me or not
as long as I get fed.
Sometimes I tease them to feed me,
then turn up my nose at what I get.

Dog: Making the acquaintance of babies,
I allow them to pull my hair.
I do not like it,
but I allow it, for
I am the dog.

Cat: When babies come into the house,
I try to *vanish*.
Babies are crazy!
Babies *sit* on you!

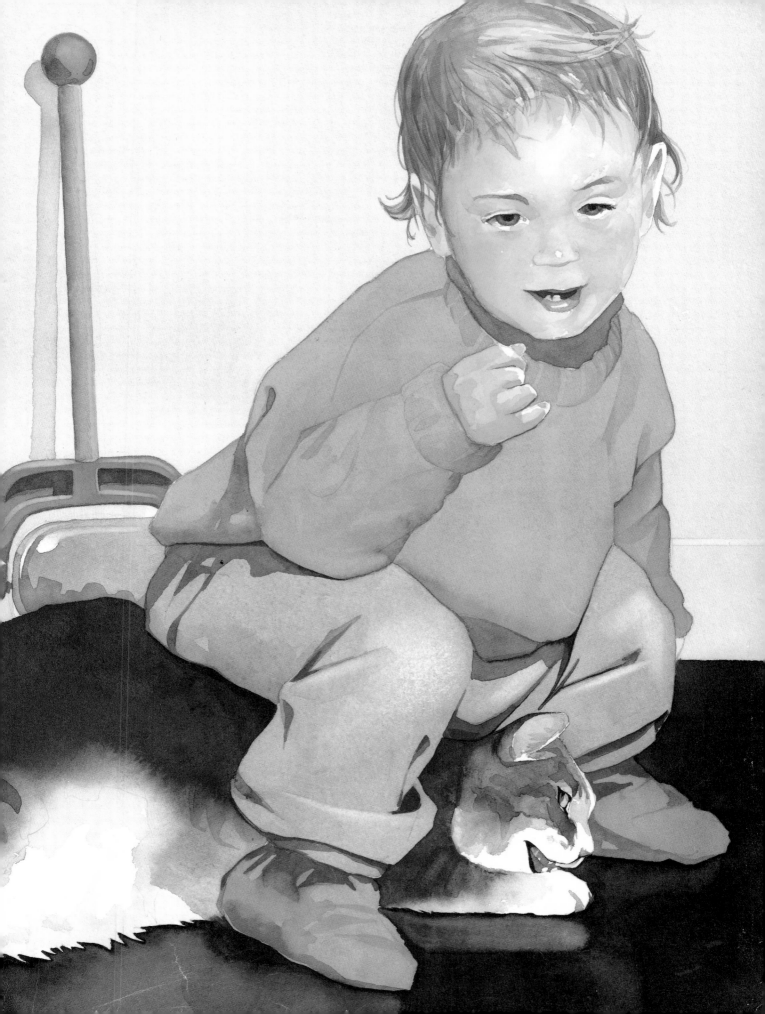

Dog: I am brave as I bark
      to frighten the burglar
      disguised as a U P S man,
      or the kidnapper who pretends to be a
         bicyclist
      wanting a drink of water.

Cat: Strangers are just fine.
      If I feel like a lap, I feel like a lap.
      Why should I care what *they* feel like?

DOG: I sleep all day in order to stay rested,
in order to be alert
when it is my duty to bark.

CAT: I sleep all day
in order to stay awake all night
on mouse patrol.

DOG: After I sleep all day,
I sleep all night, for
I am the dog.

CAT: Cats work hard.
When people and dogs are asleep,
I never stop hunting mice.
In the absence of mice,
I hunt pieces of paper, paper clips, or
rubber bands.

DOG: When I walk in the country, I chase rabbits,
them,
butterflies,
trucks,
and sticks, for
I am the dog.

CAT: When I want to go through a door,
I paw at it and meow.
When they finally open the door,
I don't want to go through it anymore.

DOG: When I smell something wonderful,
I roll in it.

CAT: Every now and then
I decide to act frightened.
From a deep sleep I leap
suddenly into the air,
then run off and hide somewhere.

DOG: I am nervous
       when I hear thunder,
       firecrackers, or guns,
       and nothing *they* say
       will comfort me.

CAT: Nothing frightens me.
       It's not that I'm brave.
       It's just that nothing
       frightens me.

DOG: When I walk in town, I sniff at fireplugs,
       telephone poles,
       fences,
       hedges,
       and other dogs, for
       I am the nose.

CAT: All day long, when I'm awake,
　　　I watch birds from the top of the
　　　　　bread box
　　　in the pantry window.
　　　If I listed all the birds I've ever seen,
　　　the list would go on for a thousand pages.

DOG: I scratch fleas
　　　suddenly and ferociously.

CAT: Don't touch me! for
　　　I am the cat.

DOG: When I swim in the pond,
    I bark at minnows.
    Then I shake water on you, for
    I am the dog.

CAT: I keep myself clean.
    What if the president dropped by?

DOG: I like chasing a ball.
      It amuses me
      when *they* beg to get it back.

CAT: The VCR is warm.
      It is my bed-in-the-house, for
      I am the yawning cat.

DOG: I like my ears scratched.
I like praise.
I cannot bear it when *they* use that tone
of voice.
I am ashamed, for
I am the dog.

CAT: The dog amuses me.
He cares about what people think!
I wash his muzzle.

DOG: I pretend-nip the cat when she washes me.

CAT: Dogs are nervous and well-meaning.
It is well-known that cats
are at the same time
independent,
selfish,
fearless,
beautiful,
cuddly,
scratchy,
and intelligent.

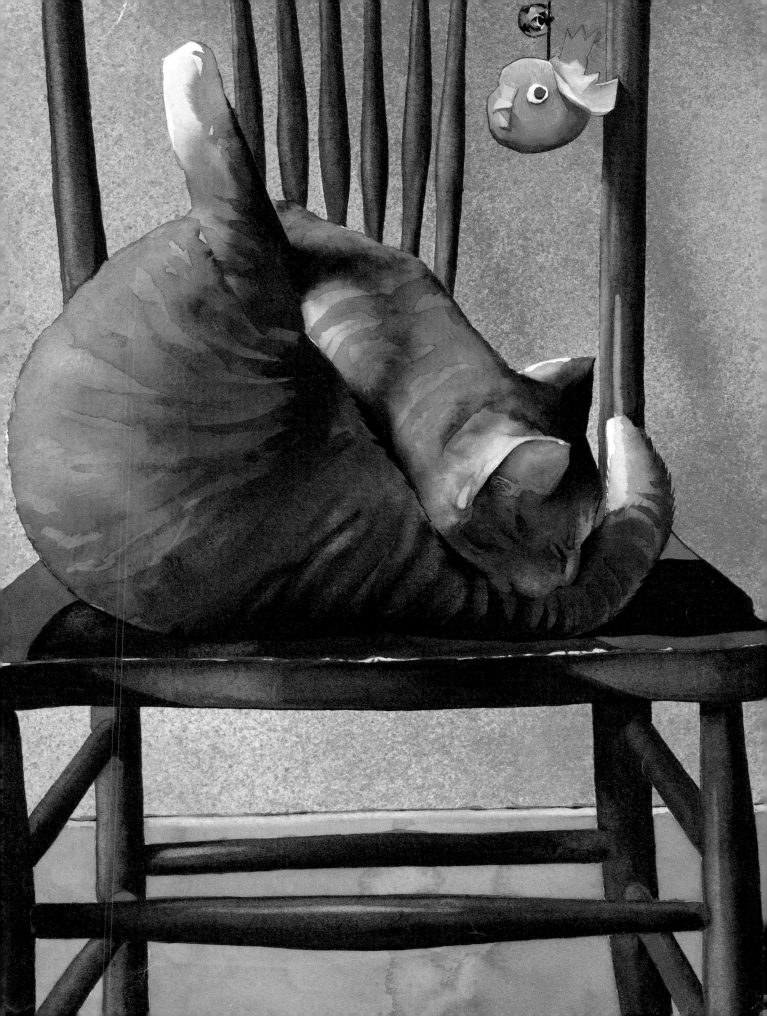

Dog: Cats just don't *care*.
Only a dog
is at the same time
dignified,
guilty,
sprightly,
obedient,
friendly,
vigilant,
and soulful.

CAT: I leap for his throat!
I hurl myself at his muzzle,
which is the same size as I am.
After a while he bows.

DOG: Cats are weird.

CAT: I walk away
with my tail in the air, for
I am the cat.